'The Cat and the Crafty Canary'

They'd been sitting silently watching each other for over an hour now. The canary on its high perch in its large circular cage and the cat sitting stretched out along the chair arm. There was no one else in the room; the homeowners were away at work.

It was the canary that blinked first: "What are you looking at me like that for?" He asked nervously.

In a sleepy voice the cat replied: "because I want to eat you!"

" Once the conversation had started it couldn't end just like that and anyway the canary thought of himself as a bit of a psychiatrist. " I appreciate your candour but you do realise you'd be very unpopular and would probably get booted out of the house if you had your wish"

The cat sighed miserably, "Yes you're quite right; it's just that I can't seem to do anything right for them these days. She never throws the ball of wool for me now and he keeps treading on my tail, quite deliberately I think, and they're never grateful when I've been out hunting all night and drop a dead mouse on their bed. I get no thanks for it!"

"Oh dear we are feeling sorry for oneself aren't we" said the canary as he started his perch into a slow swing.

The cat was easing himself into a right old sulk, the kind which could last for days or even weeks. "It's alright for you, you can do no wrong; as soon as they hear your chirpy whistling they're all over you."

The canary stopped swinging and realised he had to do something or things could get violent, there was a lot of pent up resentment about to break out.

Wearing his consultant psychiatrist's hat the wise bird asked the cat what was really the matter…deep down.

The cat was clearly embarrassed but he'd gone this far so he threw caution to the wind and came out with it: " Look if you want to know the truth, I'm not what I appear to be.   At heart I would like to sing and whistle like you and fly about, but all I can do is slink around and arch my back and meow and…well, I'm absolutely fed up with it, at times I feel quite suicidal and more than once have thought of contacting the Samaritans. I could throw myself off a bridge but I'd have to do it nine times.

The canary had to think. He'd started this and now realised he'd opened a right can of worms, so to speak. He concluded that to empathize was the best way to proceed for the benefit of his patient (for he now saw the cat as his responsibility).

" Would it help you to know that I've dreamed more than once of being a big strong hunter like you, free to roam about all night and to come and go as I wished." A sudden idea flashed through his mind: Hey! Suppose…no…it wouldn't work…"

"Go on." said the cat, desperate for any assistance.

The canary jumped in with both feet: "what about if I could teach you to whistle and in return you were to teach me to hunt in the dark…you know… it would be our secret."

The cat perked up as he realised the potential of the suggestion…"and fly, I must learn to fly as well…"

This would not be easy, thought the canary but he agreed, saying: "okay… we'll try but flying is all in the mind, it's like learning to float and swim, it's all about confidence. You'll keep trying and failing and then one day you're off and away."

It was agreed that as soon as the people left for work the cat would open the cage and release his new friend to start their practise sessions.

Next day came and after several failed attempts the cat got the cage door open and the bird flew out. Every day for a month they worked at their new scheme. At the end of that period the cat had learned to warble by inserting a marble into his mouth and the canary was able to spring around on the floor like a cat. Then it was time for flying lessons. The canary was able to demonstrate his fantastic aerobatics, whirling and swooping and diving, turning away from the big mirror over the fireplace, a split second before impact,

coming to rest, breathlessly on the lampshade and inviting the cat to try, and saying: "don't forget it's all about confidence and timing, it's all in the timing!"

The tidy room was soon looking the worse for wear with broken ornaments scattered about.

With difficulty the cat managed to leap up in stages onto the top of the open door and then took off, aiming for the big mirror, anything that crazy bird could do; so could he!

This was easy…the cat was away, his impetus carried him across the room and then he

Reached the big mirror. The glass shattered with an almighty crash and shards scattered all over the floor.

The cat had a wicked headache and knew he had to do a bunk.

When the owners came back and saw the mess they went hunting for the culprit. He was nowhere to be seen. The Canary's door was wide open and the bird it seemed had flown.

Next they went to the cat's bed and there was the canary, stretched out, fast asleep and snoring contentedly, head on the pillow and with a happy smile on his face, one leg crossed over the other. The cat had taken off and was looking for another home after being outsmarted by a clever bird.

******

'Little Nelson *his story'

Little Nelson

(The difficult newcomer and the butter pot)

Little Nelson exploded into our lives like a firecracker, jumping and fizzing and sparking all over the place, causing all sorts of mayhem.

He was a pocket-sized, giant with a heart as big as a lion and his frustrations were hilarious to watch as he regularly attempted to do great things that, by virtue of his size, he was totally incapable of doing. I'll explain this later. Right from the first moment he joined us **I became number three in the pecking order.** I know this is a sign of weakness, **you should always be in charge of the dog but I know my limits!**

He must have been about three years old at the time and we had him for over ten fun-filled and action packed years until his death from a form of leg paralysis that our vet says is quite common in this breed. I carried him out to the car and for his final journey and there was never a murmour as I passed him over to the young lady vet's assistant. He turned his head back to me and we locked eyes … and it was as if he knew this was the end of our road together. I walked away and left him to die, the betrayal deep within me! There was never a more travelled dog, from the north and south to the east and west coast, we covered them all. This story is not meant to be a lovesick tribute to a simpering lap dog. Nelson was none of those, but a remarkable Jack Russell and a great companion, but you had to earn his friendship and it wasn't easy, especially for me.

I had many problems with him in the early days, trying to break him in to my commands, as he was such a wild thing with a mind of his own. He was so self-willed and stubborn and distrustful of me that I thought it would never work.

As a boy I'd had a German Shepherd dog (called Rob) from a pup and used to let him swim for a stick each morning in a nearby lake, before I went to school. He and I had hit it off right from the beginning and he would obey my commands unquestioningly. Not so with Little Nelson. He'd ignore me and carry on doing his own thing as if I didn't exist. I soon found out that Jack Russell's are a breed apart and can be awkward little monsters at the best of times, but superb friends for all that. If ever a dog could be described as a 'Man's-Man' then that was Little Nelson. But he liked the ladies of his own species and the human variety too and they certainly loved him. My wife Margaret forged an immediate bond with him as she fed him each day. He would follow her around the house and rarely left her side, becoming her shadow-protector. He knew whenever a butter pot was about to be emptied and it would then be his. He used to nudge me forcefully to one side to keep me well away as he suspected I was trying to muscle in on his 'special treats.' Of course he wasn't to know it, but I would say in my own defence that I've never licked a butter pot in my life!

****

Little Nelson

'(It's a Small Dog's Life)

The kids had grown up and were off doing their own thing. Uncaring as kids are at that age, they'd left a vacuum, a big hole in the home. Where there'd been a constant buzz and lively chatter each day, there was now just the two of us, man-and-wife, to rattle around an empty house. That is to say, when we were there, for most weekends, weather permitting we'd pack our bags and be off on our four hour drive, to our retreat, a cottage in the Scottish Borders, in a little village called Norham, on the banks of the tidal River Tweed.

This is a wonderful, enchanted place, with an old bridge crossing the fine salmon-river that links England with Scotland. It's famous as the spot where Robert the Bruce' once laid siege to the castle on the hill overlooking the village. And the castle inspiration for Sir Walter Scott's epic poem 'Marmion'

Anyway it's such good walking country around Northumberland, the Scottish Borders and the coastal areas that we thought it would be nice to get a dog. We've had dogs before, and since, (another Jack Russell we named Big Nelson 2 with longer legs) and even a cat when we first married, but this time we knew we didn't want a pup. Perhaps a dog with two or three years under *his* belt (yes, you've spotted it, we wanted a male dog) and *he* had to be fairly small, for our smallish house…and short haired. We'd a good idea which breeds to consider. Also our daughter Karen still came back home to stay with us from time to time and she suffers from Asthma, so we had to be careful not to leave too many dog hairs about.

Well, we went along to our nearest animal rescue centre and after explaining our quest, walked along the isle between the two rows of tall steel wire cages.

There were several noisy dogs in each cage, all baying wildly for attention. Karen was with us on this special occasion to help us make a reasonable choice (teenagers can be very patronising to parents).

It was very disappointing! In a matter of minutes we'd seen lots of dogs, but although many jumped out at us and 'said take me home' none seemed quite right for us. Reluctantly we told the smiling young kennel maid we were unable to make a choice and would have to try again another time. However she persuaded us to do another walk-by. We did so without much enthusiasm. There were dogs of all shapes and sizes but we were out of luck. Then amongst the noisy Dalmatians, the boxers, the fussy Spaniels and the beautiful big-eyed Labradors we spotted a quiet Jack Russell. He was of the short-legged variety. His colouring was solid tan over the whole of his back but from neck to chest he was pure white.

He'd been inside the kennel at the rear of the cage, coming out eventually to see what all the commotion was about and was now strutting up and down in front of the others with his head held high…as high at it could go…being attached to a ridiculously low body with his belly only inches from the floor. Even so, in his own quiet way he had a certain presence and I remarked he was like a general inspecting his troops on parade. We asked for a collar and lead and Karen did a walk test up and down the centre of the isle with the other dogs looking on. They all went silent as he passed, again raising his head imperiously. We took him home without hesitation and called him Little Nelson. It seemed he had chosen us!

From the moment he arrived he became one of the family.

Once the car was in the drive and we'd shut the gate he leapt out of the back and immediately started dribbling a large round stone back between his legs. I was ordered by two enraptured females to go out and buy him a ball. He was in control from that point on.

******

Little Nelson

(A shock for Little Nelson)

We have never been an overly sentimental family and we both agreed that Nelson ought to sleep on a thick cushion in his own wickerwork chair downstairs in the conservatory, rather than upstairs with us. This was fine until we were woken up about two o-clock the first morning by a loud howling. It was Nelson. He was letting us know he was unhappy with his sleeping arrangements. We both went down and checked. He stopped his howling, sat up and wanted to play. I was tired and I wasn't having any of this. It was not as though he was a young pup. He was warm and dry and had plenty of fresh water. What more could he want. I read him the riot act and said goodnight again. 'That ought to shut him up.'

Wrong! We were just getting off to sleep again when he started up his howling once more. This time Margaret was first to get up to try and sort him out. After a few minutes later she came back to bed and we both drifted off into an uneasy sleep, half expecting to be awakened once more by his bawling. It didn't happen and next morning I asked Margaret how she had eased his distress and mine as well. 'It was easy!' She said. 'I just switched the radio on and left him listening to some smooth night-time music on the BBC.

This was to be the trick whenever we left him alone for any length of time, day or night. He wasn't choosy, highbrow or jazz or even Rock and Roll, he liked 'em all. He even got addicted to the Archers on Radio four. We switched the wireless on low and never had a problem.

We'd only had Little Nelson for a few days and he was incredibly lively and full of fun so we decided to take him into the Derbyshire Dales for a good long walk, to try and slow him down a bit, but we got more than we expected and it nearly cost him his life.

He was good as gold in the car journey and must have known he was in for an exciting time. We parked up and as we walked along the canal towpath we thought he could be let off the lead.

That was mistake number one. He wandered along, taking in all the strange new scents, but always kept looking back to make sure my wife and I were still within hailing distance, (this appealing habit never left him). It was a very bright sunny day in the height of summer and every inch of the Canal was covered in a smooth floating weed that grows into a solid thick green carpet, reminiscent of water buttercup.

Deep in a valley we were busily admiring the spectacular scenery of the hillsides on both sides and Nelson had stopped behind us, totally absorbed in a patch of foliage that had probably been rubbed by a fox or a rabbit or some nocturnal animal. We weren't concerned though, as there was a short footbridge over the canal, just passed the old pump house and a few hundred yards in front of us, where we would cross over to the other side and retrace our steps. It would be no trouble for Nelson to do the same. Wrong!

Once over the other side we called to Nelson as we drew abreast of him. He still had not moved and was sniffing all around the bush in a very animated fashion.

I called out to him and he immediately turned his head our way. He had a very panicky expression and suddenly took a great leap across the canal to join us. There was a tremendous splash as he mistook the water for solid ground. They say that all dogs can swim instinctively but we realised that our little dog had never been in water in his short life, as he sunk and the waterweed closed in again, completely sealing every inch of the surface.

It was now my turn to panic and I dashed pell-mell back over the footbridge to stand breathless at the point where he had leapt in. There was no sign of him and I was convinced that my carelessness had cost him his life. I scanned the weed but there was no sign of him.

He had gone to a watery grave! I walked back across the bridge, shaking my head sadly, to rejoin my horrified wife, who had seen no sign of him since he'd crashed down and gone under. It was then I noticed a small outlet, virtually hidden, well beneath the bank side, where the canal water rushed out to join the fast flowing River Derwent (running parallel and at least ten feet below).

A bit of old wooden branch had drifted along and was stretched across the narrow entrance and there-shivering like a drowned rat and clinging bravely to the flimsy perch, was Little Nelson. He had somehow managed to travel underwater and grasp this last chance of survival, before he was washed down to the rocky-river and his death.

We took him home and introduced him to a warm drink of tea in his bowl. He took to it greatly after that and whenever he heard the magic word 'Tea' from either of us, he would sit bolt upright on his hind legs, wave his paws madly and howl for his own drink, and he had to have his very own mug of tea. Offer him tea out of anything other than his favourite mug and he would snort derisively and turn away.

We had been told at the Rescue Centre that our Jack Russell had been owned by an old lady who'd found him too lively and couldn't give him the exercise he needed. We also believed that at sometime or other he'd had a bad experience, probably being beaten by a man, for he was suspicious of me and all my attempts to break him into our ways would end in failure.

Often when I called him he would throw a 'deaf un' pretend he couldn't hear me. This was exasperating and I'm sure a clever dog trainer could have told me where I was going wrong. All my shouting had no effect and it came to a head when I verbally chastised him for ignoring my command and he barred his teeth. From his defiant look and the enormous ridge that came up on his back, making him look for all the world like a miniature camel, I knew he was telling me: "Yes, you just try it pal and I'll have your legs off!" My wife Margaret was watching and said I would never master him like that; "he didn't know me yet. I had to win him over by psychology. If I'd carried on trying to control him by noisy instructions he would never have given up and I would have been the loser." So I relented and decided to take him on a good walk, in order that we could get to know one another better. This was to be the best thing I ever did and was the first of many long walks we had together over the years, around the local countryside. With Nelson off the lead it was always a very pleasant experience. Unlike walking with fellow humans, no conversation is required and you are free to wander, enjoying all the sights and smells and sounds of the countryside. It was like being a kid again when the sunny days stretched out endlessly. I like to think we built up a mutual respect, on these marathon treks for he looked forward to them enormously and used to bring me his lead. Needless to say he never barred his teeth at me again.

****

Little Nelson

(*Little Nelson meets the Rottweiler*)

We've had several dogs over the years and as every dog lover knows, like humans, they each have their own very special characters, quirks and foibles, but for fun and adventure and sheer joy of living we have never known one like Little Nelson.

He got into so many scrapes through his curious nature and didn't seem to understand that he was only a little bit of 'doggy nonsense on legs' a nonsense that lasted with us for well over a decade.

It was only a week or so after he'd had a narrow escape from a watery grave so we weren't prepared for what happened next. We thought he would have learned his lesson. Wrong!

My wife and I were strolling along a quiet country lane with just the odd cottage dotted here and there, and enjoying the sunshine and the glorious Peak District atmosphere.

Nelson was on a lead and we thought we had control (our mistake) for just as we came round a bend in the lane we approached a stretch of Copper Beech hedging.

This marked the boundary of a cottage garden and there was an open gateway just in front of us. We hadn't noticed Nelson's head was pointing skyways as he picked up a scent. Then without warning he slipped his collar and shot off, bolting into the open gateway like a rocket.

I had no choice but to follow him to the sound of furious, deep throated growling.

I was convinced the house owner was keeping an angry bear and just hoped it was securely chained up.

The man of the house opened his door just as I raced up, urgently calling out, to restrain my dog.

I was already far too late. The growling animal was not chained up and Nelson was a good three-foot off the ground as he'd leaped for the throat of a full-grown Rottweiler! It's own neck was thicker than Nelson's middle and it was determined to eat the cheeky little whippersnapper that had invaded it's territory.

They'd locked jaws and once again I was convinced I was witnessing the very last day of Little Nelson's short life.

The Rottweiler's owner was a very brave man. He came out shouting and wielding a great cudgel that he promptly crashed down on his dog's rump - to no avail!

The monster was not going to be deprived of its dinner. I was instructed to grab the other end of the coupling whilst he took a firm grip on his beast's manically twisting hindquarters.

I did as I was bid; after all, I had nothing to lose – except perhaps my life! We both tugged and pulled, it was a right royal tug of war and I was on the smaller end with my unprotected hands precariously close to those great slavering gnashers! Both dogs had their teeth completely interlocked, with gums well forward, exposing skeletal jawbones. We heaved like the devil but couldn't free them. Finally it was a sharp tap on the Rottweiler' snout, by the owner's hefty club, which separated the two warring animals. I quickly made my humblest apologies and hustled Nelson away. Back on terra firma the wicked little trouble-maker just shook his head and seemed quite proud and none the worse for his experience: but after that we bought him a leather full-body harness that we nicknamed his 'gun-belt.'

Try as he might he never managed to slip free of this encumbrance and wore it as a badge of honour.

I should hasten to add that in spite of this incident, Nelson usually got on well with other dogs and really liked people, especially children. He loved being fussed over.

He was always a shameless seeker-of-attention and would sit upright, back on his hind legs and wave his paws like mad if a passer-by showed him the slightest interest. I have several of these incidents to recount later, where Nelson seemed to be auditioning for 'The X Factor.'

****

Little Nelson

(Performing an extraudinary trick)

Like many dogs, his favourite sport was chasing a ball.

We would often stand at the top of a very steep grassy slope looking out over acres of grassland in the grounds of a large country estate near our home and from there I would throw his ball as far into the distance as possible.

I don't think Nelson's eyesight was brilliant. He would be avidly watching my arm movements, as I prepared to throw the ball and sometimes I would trick him so he would go tearing halfway down the hill and then stop and race back.

When I did let the ball go he would not always know where it landed, but that was when the fun began, especially for us watchers. He would get to the bottom of the hill where the ground levelled off to flat meadow. This is when he would perform an extraordinary trick that I have never seen other dogs do. Systematically he would quarter the ground as he followed his nose and his keen sense of smell. He would sometimes spend ten or fifteen minutes criss-crossing the area and working really hard until he located the ball, stopping every so often to look back to see if we were still there, waiting for him. We got the distinct idea he'd once been abandoned and was making sure it didn't happen again. In the whole time we had him he never once gave up on a ball and I would get tired long before him.

****

Little Nelson

(*Caught coursing a hare*)

Like many Jack Russell's Nelson was a keen rabbit chaser and one day we took him to a large woodland estate in North Nottinghamshire, where there is a lot of old trees and bushes for a lively dog to explore. We'd set out our picnic in a grassy open space and were having a quiet moment or two and hadn't notice Nelson sloping off as he investigated the many interesting scents. He didn't usually go far away from us and we didn't think he could come to much harm in this environment. The afternoon slipped by as we lazed in the sun and then it was time for us to depart. Where was Nelson? We both wandered about calling his name but he was nowhere to be seen. We should have tethered him to a tree but it didn't seem fair to do this, as he loved his freedom. Here was nearly 4000 acres of rolling countryside, forest and heath. It would be impossible to search the whole area.

Eventually we had no choice but to give up, and go home without him. On the way home we stopped off at a police station and reported our loss, in the forlorn hope that someone may have spotted him and taken him in hand. I explained where we had been for the afternoon and said that our dog was wearing a full harness with an inscribed nametag securely fastened on. The tag also bore our address and phone number.

Two days later the phone rang and a policeman told us the little varmint was safe and well and was snug and secure in centrally heated kennels and having the time of his life. He'd been spotted coursing a hare on a nearby private estate by the gamekeeper, who had actually raised his shotgun to his shoulder to fire when he noticed the harness and realised the dog was not a stray. He managed to grab the little blighter and put him in with the estate dogs. We could collect him just as soon as we liked.

After his near drowning escapade at the canal we knew that Nelson would never be a great swimmer. They say all dogs can swim and Nelson liked water, as we were soon to find out when we took him on our travels around the Scottish Borders and Cumbria. But, and it was always a big but, he would only attempt very shallow water such as the rock strewn rivers and streams to be found along the Pennine Way. These were his delight and once he'd got his feet wet it was a struggle to get him to leave. He would go into his 'I'm deaf' routine and we would have to physically lift him out and put him in the car.

It was our first Autumn with him when we booked into a hotel overlooking Lake Windermere. On the phone we checked if dogs were accepted. The receptionist had no qualms: 'Dogs do not steal from hotel rooms!' We were told. So Nelson was able to pack his bags and come along with us for the long weekend break. The Room had superb views over the lake and we had a four-poster bed. Nelson had his own bed that fitted snugly under the four-poster. This was fine and he slept well. We were going to leave him in the hotel room for a short while as we took a walk through the busy shopping crowds (no place for a dog).

We came back to hear such a racket going on inside our room that it sounded like a party was going in full swing. We opened the door to see two giggling young women, room cleaners, having a merry old time, doing a tug of war with Little Nelson. He had one end of a snow-white bath towel firmly in his teeth and the girls were hanging on to the other end, pulling for all they were worth, half in and half out of the adjoining bathroom.

We had interrupted the mother of all battles and Little Nelson was not about to give in!

****

Above: Strenketh Park near Kirkby Stephen. One of Little Nelson's favourite paddling haunts

****

Biscuit and Stagger

'The almost, true tale of a blind dog called Biscuit and his peg-leg friend called Stagger'

We met, quite by accident, seven years ago, on one of those hot summer days, when the mere act of walking seems to drain all the energy out of your legs.

I was taking my usual woodland walk before tea and had just stopped to rest, when I heard it.

"Pick up your feet, you clumsy oaf! You almost flattened me just then."

This voice didn't sound quite human. I looked around, but was quite alone, no sign of man or beast. After shaking my head and thinking I'd imagined it, I carried on my way.

Then I heard it again:

"Oh, bother, I'd have been better off hitching a ride on a three-legged donkey, I'll never get home at this rate."

There it was again, I thought I'd caught a touch of the sun.

The sound was now coming into my left ear. Anyway, deciding to humour it, I asked the obvious question:

"Who are you, and where are you?"

"No, you first: what's your name and why are you wearing those dark glasses?"

Okay. I gave in. "Can't you see my white stick- I'm a blind Jack Russell dog, named Biscuit and I object to giving anybody a free ride."

The voice in my left ear began a long choking laugh,

"Oh dear we are a right pair, there's you: a blind-dog-Biscuit and here's me, a flea with a wooden leg called Stagger."

I was curious, he was obviously an articulate flea that chance had blown across my path, but how had he come to lose a leg?

I'm a sucker for a story and I just had to know more.

"How'd you lose your leg? Been in the wars have we? Or were you born like it?"

I began to wish I'd never asked, as he bent my ear back and started on his tale.

"I'm not your average fly-by-night, I had ambitions to become the star attraction in the Flea Circus. I was doing a very dangerous reverse triple leap and backwards somersault, from the high wire, when I fell and landed awkwardly. There was no safety net and although I had the best attention money could buy, my damaged leg had to be amputated. I'd fallen very heavily and the Harley Street surgeon said I was lucky to be alive." He sighed, "Now I hobble about with a wooden leg.

Part two-Biscuit and Stagger.

As we ended part one, Stagger, the crippled flea is explaining his life story to Biscuit the blind Jack Russell…

Luckily I was kept on at the flea circus as chief coach, and in all modesty I've trained the best fleas in the land.

I cut him off there; I was getting hungry. Explaining I lived alone in a small cottage I said: you're welcome to join me for a spot of tea old fellow."

Over a cup of Earl Grey and a toasted teacake, my new friend continued with his amazing, life-story.

"I hail from a long line of artistes. My family have always been go-getters, my great, great, grandfather rode with Buffalo Bill in his Wild West Show and dad performed with the Great Fleadiny of 'Barnum and Baily.' My younger sister 'Licea' is a top model on the cat-walk: she's even appeared on 'Big Brother' but had to leave early: couldn't stand all the back-biting that went on" He hesitated, "You say you're completely blind?"

I nodded, "correct! Glaucoma- nothing can be done."

Later, he explained his great idea: To all intents and purposes it would be just you, performing on your own in the circus: doing impossible tricks for a blind dog.

"I could become your manager, teaching you, sword-swallowing: fire-eating and my favourite trick that always brought the house down: riding a bicycle, through a series of road cones. I would be with you, whispering instructions from behind your ear, every step or rather pedal of the way."

Despite my objections: *that you can't teach an old dog new tricks,* we decided to give it a try. After much hard work and bruising falls; he introduced me to Bertie Miles Circus as: The Amazing Blind Biscuito.

We travelled the world together, and now he's sadly gone…buried under the old apple tree in my garden. I mow the grass around his grave every week to keep the cats away.

As 'Biscuito' I carried on for a while with an apprentice flea but it was never the same, so I finally retired to write a story…his story, I thought the world should know.

****

Naja The Bear

"Money is your god Marcel and you gamble to get it, but I need only to live a simple life. My injury means we can no longer perform together on the high wire so I suggest we go our separate ways. We don't really like one another and you will be free to seek your fortune. What do you say brother? We can divide the money our father left us."

Marcel smirked contemptuously. "As usual you are right Andre, you have only yourself to blame for your damaged leg and I cannot carry a cripple."

The brothers duly split up and Marcel sought out the Italian circus owner Cecil Brinchello for advice on performing a solo act.

"Andre my dear friend, we have known each other a long time and circus is in your blood as it is in mine, bring me a new theme for a clever animal act and we'll try it out in the Big Top. But no cruelty mind! Brinchello's Renowned Circus is loved by all for its kindness to animals and I will not have its name besmirched."

Travelling through India in search of a suitable animal the ex-trapeze artist chanced across a tribe of poor Kalandar Nomads and discussed his quest. The leader said he could supply a healthy beast for a price. Andre was sickened to discover the animal in question was tied to a post in the compound.

It was a full-grown male Sloth Bear called Naja and in shocking condition. There was a ring through a hole in its snout that the chief proudly explained was made with a red-hot poker.

Now a sturdy rope linked it to the wooden stake rammed deep into the ground. Children were mercilessly pelting it with stones, forcing it to stand upright and dance. Indian Flute and Sitar music played loudly in the background; Naja's eyes were glazed, his coat was matted and dull and there was congealed blood around his swollen muzzle from the constant tugging of the rope. He was clearly in pain from the mindless torture.

"Stop it! Stop that at once" shouted the enraged visitor. "How much to buy?"

Slyly the nomad rubbed his palm and indicated many Rupees. "He velly cheap…you buy now?"

Andre promptly bartered the deal and found a local vet to check out the animal for Tuberculosis and malnutrition. The vet confirmed Naja was clear of disease although seriously underweight and in need of several vitamin injections before a long journey could be considered.

All its teeth had been removed to stop it biting and both feet had been damaged through having to hop about on red-hot coals as part of its training. Andre had an affinity with animals and had studied the art of *'Horse Whispering'* so was able to relax the great bear swiftly through simple kindness. Returning home and waiting for the beast to pass through quarantine the new keeper was not idle but with the help of an electronics wizard he explained his plan.

Several months later he demonstrated his new act to his circus boss. It was quite simple and called "Naja the Incredible Driving Bear."

The bear sat at the driving wheel of an open electric car remotely controlled by Andre out of sight of the audience and appeared to drive through a town-set, within the Big Top Arena.

A clown dressed as a policeman would halt the car at a level crossing and then wave it on after several other clowns dressed as schoolchildren had passed by

After the rehearsal the circus folk stood up and applauded enthusiastically and Cecil Brinchello had no hesitation in booking the splendid act. Naja now had a shiny coat and was fed daily on fresh fish and other delicacies.

No ill treatment was involved and he showed all the signs of loving his new life and enjoying the applause. Soon many children were dragging their parents to see the wonderfully clever Naja. The bear was a star attraction wherever Brinchello's Circus appeared. Then Marcel returned.

"I heard you were struggling on without my guiding hand! Well really Andre…? A silly Bear Act indeed! How low can you sink, once we were the 'Bravade Brothers' courageous champions of the Trapeze, have you no pride?"

Andre was taken aback but could tell from his brother's dilapidated clothing that his search for wealth had failed. He was on his uppers and the bear keeper was touched with sympathy.

"Drinking and gambling again?"

"Surely a man needs a few pleasures! I have watched your performance and I could be the policeman? What do you say brother, we were a good team once, you and I?"

Against his better judgement Andre relented and the two men were reunited. Marcel threw himself into his part, fully intending to be the dominant partner once more. He had a baton specially made which possessed a sharp retractable blade and this he thrust surreptitiously through the bear's fur on every occasion when they were alone. This made the animal howl with pain but after a while Andre noticed the dried blood on

Naja's coat. "Can't understand it Marcel I'm sure there is no barbed wire or sharp projections anywhere near Naja's quarters?"

"You worry too much, it's probably self harm, these dumb animals get bored easily and often scratch themselves deeply in frustration!"

A crisis came during a matinee performance. Marcel the policeman arrived worse for drink and began stabbing the unfortunate bear with his baton blade when the car had broken down at the level crossing. The crowd were getting restless, suddenly the crazed animal could stand it no longer and lashed out with a giant paw knocking Marcel to the ground and then leaping on him and crushing him to death. A stunned audience watched in horror as the bear was shot and killed by the armed security guards.

After a decent interval of mourning, Andre re-opened the 'car-act' with the clowns and Naja Two: sadly retiring each evening to remove the fake bearskin from his own body.

****

Harvey Meerkat.

'...Neil Armstrong is said to have met a meercat on his famous moon landing'

Old great, great Uncle Harvey Montague-Meerkat was a liar and a cheat and more than a bit of a rogue, but I liked him for his wildness and love of adventure. To be fair he had his own moral code of a sort, but he is the only one of our family not to have his portrait hanging in the great hall of Castle Meeerkat.

Such was his high-profile infamy that my father, Tenth Baronet Montague-Meeerkat would have nothing to do with him in the later part of his life, and that is a great shame. Our family lineage has been traced back to the sixteenth century.

We originated from Eastern Europe and spread all over the world. It is not widely known but meerkats were about with the dinosoars, having wings in those days.

The wings vanished as we grew smaller and evolved into the slim-line specimens you see today. Eminent meerkat scientists say we are the true missing link, being closer to Homo Sapien than the ape or the chimpanzee.

We are all higher primates.
It is not widely known but Neil Armstrong is said to have met a meerkat on his famous Moon Landing.

Anyway let me start at the beginning. I am Anthony Montague-Meeerkat, eldest son and heir to the family fortune (a stately home set in fifty acres of beautiful Italian landscaped gardens.)

Annually we get ten thousand meerkat visitors from all over the world, Texans with their Stetson hats, Mexicans with their wide brimmed Sombreros; meekats from the Kalahari Desert, even the Scottish Clan in the bright meerkat-tartan kilts.

Now owing to Global Warming we are likely to become extinct. Our race's problem has always been our diminutive size and our distinct lack of ambition.

We could easily have surpassed humans in physical development. We meekats actually invented the wheel and it was a modest meeekat who first learned to milk a cow.

Most meeekats are content to live together in hovels deep underground and it is that aspect of their very social nature that has kept them down so to speak.

Not so old uncle Harvey. He was bright as a button and was in on the gold rush, abandoning his wife and sixteen daughters and dashing off to the Klondike to find the Motherload.

He stowed aboard the Liner Queen Mary and kept popping up and down and wandering about in the moonlight: which is said to have sparked off the first ghost story aboard that ship. He landed in New York virtually destitute and rather than seek employment there, decided to hitch hike from one state to another, meeting all the most disreputable criminals and near-do-wells you can imagine.

Eventually he crossed into Canada and arrived at the Yukon River Valley and by devious means managed to stake a false claim in Rabbit Creek as it was then (we believe it was Meerkat Creek before that.)

Some say he called out a fellow player in a poker game and shot him dead with his revolver at point blank range. He then acquired that man's claim and found untold riches. It is said he met and fell in love with Klondike Kate and it was she who betrayed him to Skookum Jim and his cronies and cost him his Bonanza claim.

It was only later that the Royal Canadian Mounties arrived to bring about a little law and order. My cousin Lydia, eldest great granddaughter of Harvey Meeekat has been to university and can speak seven languages.

Her son Calvin is a famous actor and has recently appeared on the television in an advertisement to persuade silly humans to stop clogging up our official website.

For some reason he speaks with a slightly foreign accent but is as meerkat-British has anyone else.

Anyway to get back to Harvey, after losing all his money he could have been forgiven for taking to the bottle but no, he drifted back to the states and offered his services to Buffalo Bill and his circus act, trick riding on a horse, and that was how he paid for his ticket back to England.

Somewhere my mother has an old sepia photo of him, just after he had arrived in Rabbit Creek as a starving miner. The picture shows him actually eating his own leather boots, with a touch of salt and pepper (to add flavour, of course.)

Some people believe the scene in "The Gold Rush" with Charlie Chaplin; is stolen from that incident. Those were desperate days for uncle Harvey.

Whilst with Buffalo Bill in England he tried his hand at stunt flying and grew a giant handlebar moustache to look the part. It is erroneously believed that Ormer Locklear was the first wing-walker but Harvey Meerkat beat him to it by several days. He even changed planes in mid air.

Flying was to eventually bring about his death. Like I said he had already been dare-devil wing walking, up in a two seater Sopwith Camel biplane, performing crazy handstand stunts, but what finally killed him was a free-fall flight.

He left it just too late to pull his parachute rip-cord in front of a packed open-air circus crowd and plummeted to earth. He made a crater ten inches deep.

His funeral was a great affair bringing meerkats from all over the world. The ornate gun-carriage was pulled by six jet black stallions with pure white plumes (from the circus.)

Buffalo Bill attended along with several international personalities.

A specially chosen meerkat band marched slowly in front, playing solemn music and the Meerkat Macebearer held his mace all the way in the horizontal position; which is the correct manner for a Meerkat State Funeral.

Needless to say my stuffy aristocratic parents would have none of it, saying he was beneath contempt. They thought he had brought the meerkat race into disrepute.

When the tenth Baronet goes to the great Meerkat Palace deep in the bowels of the earth and I become Eleventh Baronet, I fully intend to put old uncle Harvey's portrait
back in the great hall where he belongs. He could have been a truly great meerkat…and in his own way I believe he was.

****

Harry Riley's Potted Bio.

Born in Nottingham in 1940...
To an Irish Catholic mother and a Methodist father. 'Brought up for the first six years of my life as the other member of a single parent family and absolutely loved it... being the man of the house through the war.
I'd never met my dad as he'd joined up at the start of the war, becoming a Japanese prisoner on the Changi Railway almost immediately, eventually being found by the British Red Cross after the end of the war. He had a bullet hole in the leg and came home a gaunt stranger that I had never knowingly met before. He died in 1976.
I've two brothers and a sister and have spent the whole of my working life in the printing trade.
'Been happily married for 50+ years and with a grown up boy and girl.
Education: Sec. Mod and Nottingham College of Art
Politics: 50% Conservative. 40% Labour.: 10% open to suggestions!
My interests are gardening, writing novels, short stories, blogs, town guides and Broadcasting: have completed two mystery novels set in Nothumberland and the Scottish Borders and a third novel about a retired policeman and his private detective pal.
Favourite classics authors are Thomas Hardy, Sir Walter Scott, Charles Dickens, Conan Doyle and Rudyard Kipling. (inspired by Kipling and Longfellow as a youngster)
Favourite Books: Mayor of Casterbridge (I have known several people very like Michael Henshard), T.E.Lawrence's Seven Pillars of Wisdom
Fav. Music: easy listening classics, 50's and 60's music
Started writing 2008 : Nottingham Evening Post published my intro. bio: called "Hero's, Villains and a Pig called Monty" in 2008
Note: I often think one life is not enough!

***

Harry Riley Nottingham: Novelist, Poet, Broadcaster, Blogger

Harry Riley River Tweed
Scottish Borders

New for 2019 Novel: 'Chasing Fleeting Shadows in the Wind'
All books: Amazon Bookstore UK

email: pagedavid@icloud.com, tel: 01773 279 852
web: http//har723.wixsite.com/har723

Printed in Poland
by Amazon Fulfillment
Poland Sp. z o.o., Wrocław